Skippyjon Jones

Snow What

JUDY SCHACHNER

 DIAL BOOKS FOR YOUNG READERS
AN IMPRINT OF PENGUIN GROUP (USA) LLC

DIAL BOOKS FOR YOUNG READERS

PUBLISHED BY THE PENGUIN GROUP
Penguin Group (USA) LLC, 375 Hudson Street, New York, New York 10014

USA • Canada • UK • Ireland
Australia • New Zealand • India • South Africa • China

www.penguin.com
A Penguin Random House Company

Text and pictures copyright © 2014 by Judith Byron Schachner

Library of Congress Cataloging-in-Publication Data
Schachner, Judith Byron. Skippyjon Jones snow what / by Judy Schachner.
pages   cm   Summary: Skippyjon Jones, the Siamese cat that thinks he is a
Chihuahua dog, stars in a fairy tale set in the winter wonderland of his imagination.
ISBN 978-0-8037-3789-1 (hardcover) [1. Siamese cat—Fiction. 2. Cats—Fiction.
3. Chihuahua (Dog breed)—Fiction. 4. Dogs—Fiction. 5. Fairy tales—Fiction.] I. Title.
PZ7.S3286Sno 2014   [E]—dc23   2013044732

Manufactured in China on acid-free paper

1 2 3 4 5 6 7 8 9 10 • First Edition

Designed by Heather Wood
Text set in Lomba Medium

The publisher does not have any control over and does not assume any responsibility
for author or third-party websites or their content.

The illustrations for this book were created in acrylics and brush and ink
on Aquarelle Arches watercolor paper.

For Bertito, Matthew, Brandon, and their doggie in the mirror, Lady.
And for Baby Faith, forever held in our hearts.
As always, gracias Team Skippy. —J.S.

Skippyjon Jones loved to play
in the snow with his sisters,
Jezebel, Ju-Ju Bee, and Jilly Boo.

And this melted his mama's heart faster than a
bowlful of butter on a hot beach.

"Come on in, Mitten Kittens," called out Mama
Junebug Jones. "Time for some hot catnip cocoa."
  "With mousemallows?" begged the girls.
  "And ice cubes?" asked Skippy.
  "Don't need ice cubes, Mr. Pillow," said Mama.
"But we need to pick out a book."

"*Snow White!*" gushed the girls.
"It's our favorite fuzzy tale!"
"Fuzzy tale, shmuzzy tale,"
declared the kitty boy.

"I don't like that story,"
he said, making a disagreeable
face. Then he stomped off to
his room, carrying a tray of
ice cubes.

"Listen here, Grumpy Gums," said Mama,
following close behind.

"Your sisters have listened

to *your* favorite books

without even *once*

giving me *one*

of *those* looks!

So come have your cocoa

and do what is right.

And, who knows, Snuggle Bug,

you might **love**

the tale of Snow White!"

"Nuh-uh," said Skippy. "I don't think so."

"Suit yourself, Tater Tot," said Mama Junebug. "But you don't know what you're missing."

Oh, Skippy knew what he was missing, all right. And that was bouncing on his big-boy bed.

"Oh, I'm **Skippyjonjones**,

And I know what I'm missing,

A fuzzy white cat,

A prince . . .

and some kissing!"

"Yuck,"
said Skippy,
wiping his mouth
with the back of
his paw.

Then he popped over to his mirror and, using his very best Spanish accent, he said:

"Mirror, Mirror,

on the wall,

Who is the

handsomest

Chihuahua

of

all?"

"Why, it is
you,
Señor Skip!"
replied the Chihuahua
in the *espejo*.

"And the bravest!" declared the kitty boy as he prepared for a long journey into his closet. Then, as always, he began to sing in a *muy, muy* soft voice:

"Oh, my name is Skippito Friskito, (clap-clap)

And I know an old fuzzy tale-ito. (clap-clap)

It's got plenty of fights,

But no one wears tights,

And that's the best part, mis amigos."

(clap-clap)

Back on the couch, Junebug had begun reading to the girls.
"Once upon a pillow sat a beautiful cat princess. Her fur was
as white as snow, her eyes were as black as coal, and her whiskers
were as full as . . .

"My tummy," added Ju-Ju Bee, burping.
"That was a good story," said the sisters, running off to play.

But this wasn't the end of the story for Skippyjon Jones. It was just the beginning as he stepped into his closet . . .

. . . and into a
deep,
dark
forest.

He hadn't even gone
four paws before his
tail puffed out.

"Don't be such a scaredy-cat!" chided a fox from behind a tree.

"I'm not a scaredy-cat," hissed the *gatito*. "I am Skippito Friskito, the great sword fighter."

"Of course you are," snickered the fox. "And I'm a Chihuahua."

Skippito gave him a look that would freeze a *fuego*. Then he took off toward a light in the distance.

Over the river and through the woods, seven small *amigos* opened the door to their cozy little cottage and sniffed.

"Something is not right, dudes," said the first.

"Some dog has been chewing my *zapato*," said the second.

"And licking my *leche*," said the third.

"And sitting in
my *silla*," said
the fourth.

"And gnawing on
my *hueso*," added
the sixth.

"And tossing
my *pelota*,"
said the fifth.

"And sleeping in
my *cama*," declared
the seventh.

"Not in your bed!"
exclaimed all
the doggies.
"That stinks, dude!"

Stinky or not, there was indeed someone sleeping in the bed!
But it wasn't a dog. It was . . .

"Skippito!" hooted the poochitos,
   piling on top of their *amigo.*

"Los Chimichangos!"
exclaimed the *gatito.*
"What are you doing here?"

"We have come to free *Nieve Qué,*"
explained Poquito Tito, the smallest of the small ones.

"Snow who?" asked the *gatito.*

"Not Snow *who,* dude,"
replied Tomatillo.
"Snow What!"

Talk of *Nieve Qué* whipped the puppies
into a frenzy of froth, chanting:

"*Snow What, Snow White, Snow-ito,*
(clap-clap)
Has been cursed by a wicked witch-ito.
(clap-clap)
She sleeps in the cube,
Till she's kissed by a dude,
So pucker up, pooch,
and smooch-ito."
(clap-clap)

"I'm not kissing SNOWbody!"
declared Skippito.
"Not tonight," said all the puppies.
"But *mañana, muchacho.*"

After a tail waggin' and whisker washin', every
pup fell fast asleep dreaming of Snow What.
Every pup except Skippito.

Her fur is as **white** as the **snow** . . . .

snore, snore

Her eyes are as black as the coal . . . *snore some more*

Her nose is as **pink** as the **peony** . . . .

She is such a beautiful lady . . . .

drool

At the first bark of dawn, the *ocho* poochos were up and out in search of the frozen *princesa*.

"But why is she frozen?"
asked Skippito.

"Because," woofed Don Diego,
"she is HOT."

"*Sí*," added Poquito Tito,
"and the wicked *bruja* is not."

Hot or not, the tiny troupe would trudge through thicket and thorn for *Nieve Qué*. And nothing was going to stop them.

Not even a sleeping dragon. But it stopped Skippito.
He fainted.

"He's out cold, dudes," whispered Tío Leo.

"*Bueno,*" barked Bertito.

Then all the puppies prepared their *amigo*
for the *grande* rescue. First they dressed him.
Then they blessed him.

Salchichas salchichas,
Sausages and peaches!
Rumble tummy in the dragon's den,
One little dog with the strength of ten!
Salchichas salchichas,
Sausages and peaches!

(one more time!)

As Skippito woke up, he not only smelled the sausage, he looked like one, too.

"That's right, they're tights," scolded Poquito Tito. "And any prince who has ever rescued a *princesa* has had to wear them."
"But who's doing that?" asked Skippito, scratching his head.
"Dude," howled the doggies in disbelief, "you are!"

Suddenly a potent puff of panic
poofed out Skippito's tail and
popped his *pantalones*.

"Stand back!" warned Bertito.

Then quicker than you can say snails,
scales, and humpback whales, Skippito
rocketed up over the waking dragon.

Harradddaggggghhhhhh

roared the dragon with a shot of flame.
The poochitos loaded their slingshots
with *salchichas* and aimed straight for the
dragon's fiery *boca*.

"While we distract, it's time to act!"
shouted his *amigos* from below.

"Do your part
and melt her heart!"
barked Tomatillo, covering his
corazón with his paws.

"When put to the test, your *besos* are best!"
woofed Don Diego as he took aim.

And quicker than you can say a *beso con queso*, Skippito landed right next to the *cubito de hielo* and the frozen *princesa*.

She was a beauty all right, but the poochito was in no mood for a smooch-ito.

So at the top of his itty-bitty lungs, he shouted,

"SNOW WHAT, WAKE UP!"

Nieve Qué heard *nada*, nothing, but it scared the living fire right out of *el dragón*, and away he flew. Now *nada* stood in the way of saving the *princesa*. Except ice and a pair of fuzzy lips.

"Dude, just kiss the cube!" begged Poquito Tito again.

And so he did.

Back in their room, Ju-Ju Bee, Jezebel, and Jilly Boo were busy playing their own version of Snow White when they saw their brother walk by with an ice cube stuck to his nose.

"He's been licking ice cubes again," said Ju-Ju Bee, shaking her head.

"Yup," said Jilly Boo.
"He likes ice."

"Uh-huh," added Jezebel.
"Ice is nice."

Mama Junebug Jones was doing a crossword puzzle
at the table when her kitty boy crawled onto her lap
and buried his face in her soft, warm neck.

"Whoa," said Mama. "Some little
squeegee has a cold wet nose."
"Snow what?" asked Skippy.
"What?" said Mama.
"I love you."

"Snow what, thumbkin?"
asked Mama.
"What?" said Skippy.
"You just melted your
mama's heart."

At bedtime, the Jones girls overheard their brother bouncing on his big-boy bed, saying:

"Oh, I'm Skippyjonjones,

The bravest of knights.

But when I save a princess,

I will not wear tights!"

"What princess?" asked Ju-Ju Bee, running into his room.

"Snow What," replied the kitty boy, bouncing higher.

"Snow who?" inquired Jilly Boo.

"He meant Snow White," reasoned Jezebel.

"Snow I didn't," declared Skippy. "I said . . ."

"Good night!" called Mama from down the hall. "Skippy said 'good night.'"